Som See and the Magic Elephant

Som See and the Magic Elephant

Jamie Oliviero   Illustrated by Jo'Anne Kelly

Hyperion Books for Children
New York

Special thanks to Khamphouk and Souksavanh Thephasone

Text © 1995 by Jamie Oliviero.
Illustrations © 1995 by Jo'Anne Kelly.
All rights reserved. Printed in China.
For more information address Hyperion Books for Children,
114 Fifth Avenue, New York, New York 10011.

FIRST EDITION

1 3 5 7 9 10 8 6 4 2

This book is set in 14.5-point Palatino.
The illustrations are prepared by painting on silk using
traditional methods of batik dyeing and direct dyeing
using a brush.

Designed by A. O. Osen

Library of Congress Cataloging-in-Publication Data
Oliviero, Jamie.
    Som See and the magic elephant/written by Jamie Oliviero;
  illustrations by Jo'Anne Kelly—1st ed.
      p. cm.
    Summary: Som See helps her great-aunt prepare for death
  by finding her a good luck charm from her past.
    ISBN 0-7868-0025-9 (trade)—ISBN 0-7868-2020-9 (lib. bdg.)
    [1. Great-aunts—Fiction. 2. Death—Fiction. 3. Thailand—
  Fiction.] I. Kelly, Jo'Anne, ill. II. Title.
PZ7.04975So   1994   94-1164
[E]—dc20   CIP
                                            AC

For Nantaporn

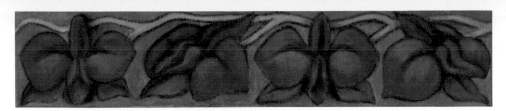

As soon as she awoke, Som See dressed quickly, then hurried to make Pa Nang's sweet tea. Pa Nang (great-aunt) had promised to take Som See to the village to participate in the harvest festival that morning. Before they departed, the old woman and her niece went into the garden to the spirit house to place offerings of incense and flowers to ensure the travelers a safe journey.

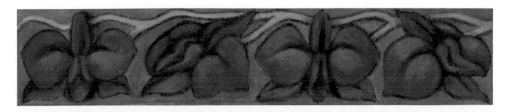

"I remember when I was your age and lived in the city," Pa Nang began as they walked along the dirt road. "There was a splendid festival to celebrate the king's birthday. He rode through the streets on the back of a great white elephant, Chang. Chang was the only white elephant we had ever seen. He had carried the king into many successful battles and was kept deep in the rainforest and brought forth only on special occasions. Wherever he went, chattering and shrieking monkeys followed him. Chang was magnificent. It was said that to touch his trunk gave a person good luck."

"Did you ever touch Chang's trunk?" asked Som See. "And have good luck?"

"Yes," the old woman replied. "But that was a long time ago. I fear such luck doesn't last a lifetime."

Som See could see that Pa Nang was troubled. But before she had time to ask more questions, they arrived in the village. The parade had already started, and Som See and Pa Nang stood at the side of the street to enjoy the drummers and dancers. At dusk they attended the shadow-puppet theater.

When the play was over, Som See and Pa Nang returned home. "Thank you, Pa Nang," the girl exclaimed. "Today was wonderful!"

The old woman smiled. Exhausted from the day's events, she retired early to her sleeping hammock.

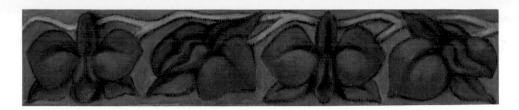

As the days passed, Pa Nang grew weak and spent much of her time in her hammock. One afternoon, as Som See sat drowsily fanning her, Pa Nang said, "I will soon leave on a journey from which I will not return to the family."

"When will you go?" Som See asked, but Pa Nang did not answer.

Som See continued to wave the fan back and forth until she thought the old woman was asleep. She was about to move away when her great-aunt's muffled whisper startled her.

"If only I could touch Chang one more time, I know my good fortune would be renewed and my journey would be peaceful." Then she drifted off to sleep.

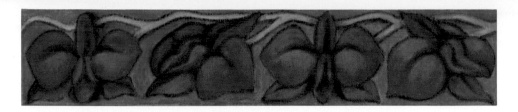

Som See walked slowly through the garden at the back of the house. What could she do to help Pa Nang as she prepared for her journey? Som See looked toward the rainforest and wondered if Chang might still be there. But how could she find him and bring him back?

Som See noticed a band of monkeys moving through the trees in a noisy game of tag. She remembered Pa Nang's story and thought they might know where she could find the white elephant. She followed the monkeys under the canopy of leaves for several minutes, but suddenly the monkeys scrambled through the branches and disappeared. Som See stopped and looked around. She was deep within the rainforest and was quite lost.

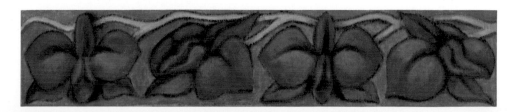

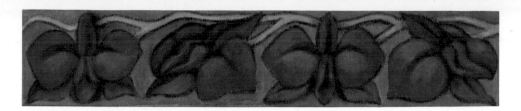

Som See walked in one direction, then another, but there were so many trees that she could not tell where she was. When she came to a stream, she sat on a stone at the water's edge and began to cry.

With a tremendous splash, a magnificent fish appeared. "What is the matter, little one? Why are you adding your salty tears to my stream?"

"I followed the monkeys in my search for Chang," she said, "and now I am lost."

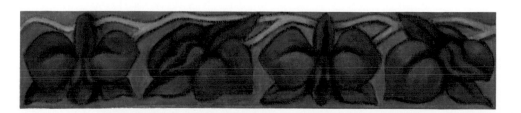

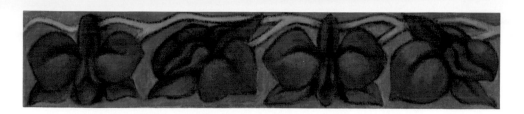

The fish said, "I am Fon Pa, the Rain Fish. Many years ago a young king built a palace in the middle of this rainforest. The palace was in honor of his white elephant who had been so gallant in battle."

"Chang!" Som See said.

"You must find the ruins of the palace," Fon Pa instructed. "And there you will find the elephant."

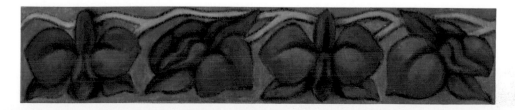

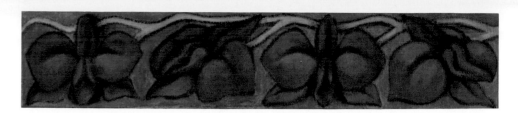

Som See continued on into the forest. She walked until her legs ached and she believed she could go no farther. Finally the trees began to thin, and she came upon a clearing. In the center stood a stone tower with a staircase of crumbling brick. Fascinated, Som See carefully climbed the broken stairs.

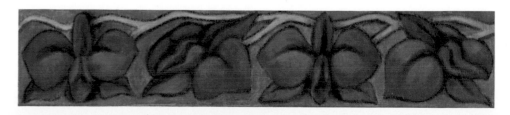

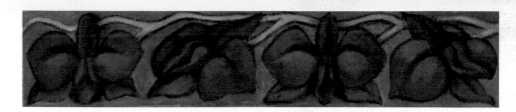

At the top of the tower there was a small chamber with a heavy stone door that stood slightly open. Som See squeezed through the doorway and looked around. She saw a brass bell in a small niche in the wall and lifted it down. Although the bell must have been sitting on the ledge for years, it shone and sparkled as if it were new. As Som See carried the bell into the sunlight, the clapper struck the side, making a high-pitched tone. Immediately Som See heard the crackling of underbrush as something large and heavy moved toward her.

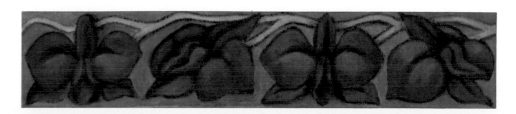

A wondrous white elephant covered with a shimmering cloth adorned with jewels stepped out of the forest.

"You have summoned me with the king's bell," he said. "I am here to do your bidding."

The elephant was magnificent, just as Pa Nang had said. Som See was so in awe of him that at first she could not speak. Finally, in a halting voice, she explained her great-aunt's request. Without another word, the huge beast raised his long trunk, wrapped it around Som See, and lifted her onto his back. Then he turned and began to walk through the jungle.

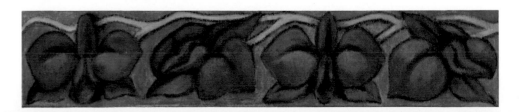

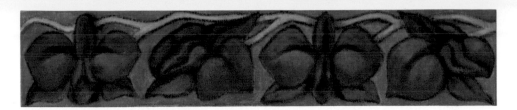

They passed Fon Pa in his stream and the chattering monkeys in the trees. Soon they approached the edge of the forest, and Som See could see the houses and the rice fields. Chang walked silently in the long grass and approached Som See's house from behind.

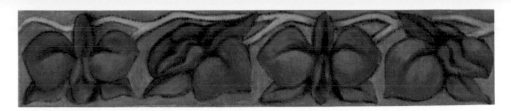

Pa Nang was still dozing in her hammock, but as Chang approached, she awoke. The elephant stood beside the porch and stretched his trunk toward her. Pa Nang lifted her hand and touched it. Then, smiling, she sank back into the hammock and sighed deeply.

"She is ready for her journey now," Chang said. The mighty elephant lifted Som See gently to the ground and then turned and disappeared in the trees.

Som See placed the bell in the spirit house as an offering for her great-aunt's safe journey.

In the morning when Som See awoke, she immediately went to her great-aunt's sleeping hammock, but it was empty. Through the doorway the little girl saw her family sitting silently in the middle of the main room. Neighbors were there with gifts of food.

Her mother beckoned her to join them. "Your Pa Nang has begun a great journey," her mother said.

I know Pa Nang's journey will be peaceful, Som See said to herself. Chang has again shared his good fortune with her.

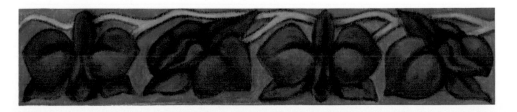

Traveling along the hundreds of *klongs*, or man-made canals, that run from the Chao Phraya River into the great flood plain of Thailand, one finds remote villages with buildings made from bamboo. Each village has a temple, a school, and a meeting place surrounded by houses. All are raised on bamboo stilts to be above the sea of mud during the wet season (six months of monsoons—heavy rain and wind) and to allow better circulation of air during the hot dry season. Air also filters through the walls of the houses, which are made from woven bamboo. Many people have a small spirit house in the yard where they place offerings to spirits to protect them on journeys, to watch over crops, and to provide safety for their house and family.

Most of the people farm the land. To honor spring planting, harvesttime, the new year, and other occasions, festivals are held in the villages. There is a carnival-like atmosphere, and traveling players often present puppet shows. The daring exploits of *kasatts*, or the regional kings of old Thailand when it was called Siam, are favorite subjects. According to one legend, a white elephant, extremely rare, carried a local king into many successful battles. The white elephant was greatly honored and became a symbol of good luck.

Over the centuries, Thai artists have perfected a number of unique ways to dye cloth. One method, called *batik*, involves applying wax to the fabric with a metal drawing pen and then immersing it in dye. No color will set where the wax adheres. The wax is then removed to reveal wondrous designs. This art form is also referred to as *pattern-resist dyeing*. It was developed in Java and northern Thailand and was first created using hemp. Contemporary batik artists use silk and cotton instead. Another traditional method is called *direct dyeing*. The artist applies dye directly to silk with a brush in much the same way a painter applies paint to a canvas. Both of these methods were incorporated in creating the illustrations for *Som See and the Magic Elephant*.